The New Kid

Written by A.M. Dassu

Illustrated by Hüseyin Sönmezay

Collins

1 First day

Mama tapped Ammar on his shoulder. "Come on, you need to get ready," she said, smiling. "We don't want to be late for your first day at your new school!"

Ammar looked out of the window and swallowed the big hard lump in his throat. He didn't want to go to a new school where he didn't know anyone or understand their language. No one would speak Arabic and he hardly knew any English – he'd never make any friends!

Ammar wanted to tell Mama he was scared but the words wouldn't come out. He didn't want to upset her, especially because this was the first time that he'd seen her excited since they'd suddenly left Syria.

Mama explained he should be happy he got into a school in England so quickly. But Ammar didn't feel lucky. He felt sad.

School in Syria was fun. He always looked forward to going and playing with his friends. Everything felt safe … until one day it wasn't.

When a bomb fell in their neighbourhood, Mama and Baba said they had to leave.

"But, Mama, you need me at home!"
Ammar said. "Who else will look after baby Yusra
when you're cooking?"

Mama laughed. "I managed to raise you without
any help. Don't worry, I'll be fine! We'd much rather
hear your stories when you get home."

The school gates loomed in the distance and
Ammar's tummy rocked. What would Mama do if he
turned around and ran back home? She wouldn't be
able to grab him in time because of the pushchair.
Or maybe he could tell Mama he felt sick? He didn't
want to run away alone in this new scary city.

"Mama, my tummy hurts." Ammar wrapped his arms around his stomach.

"You're fine!" she said, stroking Ammar's back as she walked towards school. "Come on! You're just nervous!"

Ammar dropped his shoulders and followed Mama. Nothing was going to work. He'd have to go to school.

2 School

The teacher spoke to Ammar in a strange language he guessed was English. She pointed at a chair tucked under a table where lots of children were sitting. Ammar thought this meant he should sit down, so he pulled out the chair and sat quietly. Ammar could feel all the other children staring at him. His cheeks were burning.

The teacher went to the whiteboard and the children started talking. It was a strange classroom. There were five big tables with children sitting around all of them facing each other. In Syria, Ammar sat with his friend at a desk that faced the board and his teacher.

The children at Ammar's table didn't look happy to be learning at school either. One of the girls was barely listening to the teacher as she talked to the girl next to her. Ammar would have been told off for not concentrating if he'd talked to anyone in his old school during lessons.

Everyone seemed to know each other well here. As the children chatted, Ammar felt even lonelier than he did at home. He wished he was at school in Syria with his best friend Omar, playing football together in the playground.

The teacher said something, and everyone turned to Ammar. Ammar didn't understand what she'd said so he stared at his shoes. He wanted to run and hide in the toilets, but he didn't even know where they were!

3 A different language

Ammar stared at the clock ticking on the wall, counting the minutes until three o'clock when school would finish and Mama would come to pick him up.

The teacher said something, and everyone put their hands up. Ammar turned around to see what she had said and noticed some familiar words on the board.

Ammar's eyes lit up – he could understand these words!

"Bonjour!" said the teacher. "Comment tu t'appelles? Et quel âge as-tu?"

Ammar's arms twitched and he almost put his hand up. He wanted to tell the teacher his name was Ammar, he was nine years old and he went to a French-speaking school in Syria!

But he stopped himself. If he spoke, everyone would just stare at him even more because he was different to them.

The teacher shared some animal photos and asked more questions in French. Ammar clasped his hands in his lap to stop himself from answering them.

"Miss! Miss!" one of the children at the back of the class shouted. "I know!"

In Syria, Ammar would have shouted out to the teacher, just like this girl was. But he was too shy to call out the right answer here.

Some more children put their hands up but most of them didn't know the answers.

Ammar slunk into his chair hoping the teacher wouldn't ask him anything. He'd stick out if he showed them how much French he knew.

After a while, the teacher asked the children to work at their tables. Everyone on Ammar's table looked confused.

The teacher had given out lots of different squares. Some had pictures on them and some had French words to match with the pictures.

Ammar watched everyone struggle. Should he match the words for them? He slowly moved "chat" next to the picture of a cat, and the children on his table looked surprised.

"Hey, new kid!" the boy opposite Ammar said. Ammar didn't understand so the boy reached over and tapped Ammar on the shoulder. The boy moved the picture of a horse next to the wrong word and then pointed at Ammar.

Did he want Ammar to help? Ammar guessed so.

Ammar got to work. He matched all the words in no time and sat back in his chair.

All the children at his table looked across the classroom at everyone else still working on the activity. They smiled at Ammar.

The boy with ginger hair put his hand up and shouted something to the teacher. He locked eyes with Ammar and grinned. He seemed happy that Ammar had helped their table to finish first.

"I'm Tom," he said.

"Ammar," Ammar replied, pointing at his chest.

4 Disaster

Later that morning, Ammar's class changed
into their sports clothes and headed out into
the playground.

The sports teacher asked everyone a question.
It looked like she was asking who each child wanted
to pair up with. Ammar was surprised when Tom
pointed at him.

Ammar couldn't understand the teacher's instructions, but he watched her hand out balls and racquets. It looked like they were going to play tennis. Ammar's stomach twisted as he remembered the last time Baba had taken him to the park to play tennis … It was before all the parks had become too dangerous to go to because of the war.

Tom nudged Ammar, jolting him out of his memory, and handed him a tennis racquet.

Ammar walked slowly to the other side of the net, opposite Tom. He was nervous because he hadn't played tennis for ages. If he wasn't very good any more, everyone would laugh at him.

Tom served the ball and Ammar ran to hit it over the net.

They hit the ball back and forth and Ammar breathed out. He was actually playing well! Just like he used to in Syria.

When the ball came across the net, Ammar hit it as hard as he could.

The ball shot across the playground and through the shed window!

SMASH!

Ammar looked at everyone's shocked faces.
What had he done? No one would want to be his
friend now! He imagined Mama's face when she
found out and how she'd worry about paying for it.
His eyes blurred with tears and he turned towards
the school building, running away as fast as he could.

Ammar ran to the other side of the school building and hid behind the big school bins, panting. His face was wet with tears.

He tried to calm himself. What would he do now? Had he got himself into even more trouble by running away? Should he have stayed?

Ammar jumped when he felt a hand on his shoulder.

It was Tom. "You're really good at tennis!" he said. "Let's go and play, come on!"

Had Ammar heard right? Did Tom say he was good? Ammar knew what that meant!"

Tom put out a hand to help Ammar up and smiled. He said something else that Ammar couldn't understand, but it didn't matter. Ammar could tell he was being a good friend.

They walked back to the playground and their teacher came towards them. "Ammar, Tom told me you understand French," she said in French.

Ammar nodded.

"Don't worry, you're not in trouble," she said in French. "Accidents happen all the time."

"I'm sorry for breaking the window," Ammar replied in French.

"It's fine," the teacher said in French. "But are you all right? Do you need anything to help settle in?"

"I'm OK," Ammar said in French, because now he really was. He glanced at Tom and smiled. Ammar realised that even though he didn't know any English, there were other ways he could join in and make friends. Maybe he wasn't that different to the children in England after all.

From Syria to England

home

school

sports

friends

Ideas for reading

Written by Gill Matthews
Primary Literacy Consultant

Reading objectives:
- check that the text makes sense to them, discussing their understanding and explaining the meaning of words in context
- ask questions to improve their understanding of a text
- draw inferences such as inferring characters' feelings, thoughts and motives from their actions, and justify inferences with evidence

Spoken language objectives:
- ask relevant questions to extend their understanding and knowledge
- use relevant strategies to build their vocabulary
- articulate and justify answers, arguments and opinions

Curriculum links: Geography – Locational knowledge, geographical skills and fieldwork; Languages; Relationships education – Caring friendships

Interest words: familiar, twitched, clasped, slunk, grinned

Resources: IT, atlas

Build a context for reading

- Show children the front cover of the book and read the title. Discuss who the kid might be and what he might be new to.
- Ask children to read the back-cover blurb. Discuss the question at the end. Encourage children to support responses with reasons.
- Explore children's experiences of being "the new kid" somewhere, e.g. at school, a sports club, a new house.
- Discuss children's experiences of contemporary stories. Ask what features they expect the story to have.

Understand and apply reading strategies

- Read pp2–7 aloud, using appropriate expression. Discuss how Ammar was feeling and why. Ask children how they think they would feel if they were starting at a school where they couldn't speak the language.
- Discuss any features in this first chapter that tell the children this is a contemporary story.